Millie the Magical Stone Skipper

WRITTEN BY
Olivia Polk

ILLUSTRATED BY
Vanya Liang

BIRD
UPSTAIRS

for mom & dad
and sierra ♥

Published by Bird Upstairs Books™, Seattle
www.birdupstairs.com

Produced by Girl Friday Productions

Design: Paul Barrett
Development & editorial: Devon Fredericksen
Illustrations: Vanya Liang

ISBN (hardcover): 978-1-954854-39-0
ISBN (ebook): 978-1-954854-46-8

Library of Congress Control Number: 2021919649

First edition

There once lived a rancher and his four children. It was time to go out into the big wide world. "Get good at something that will earn you a living," said the rancher to his youngsters. "Now lickety-split!"

The rancher's three boys, Boone, Billy, and Buck, were excited to make their pa proud. They had never ventured beyond the grand mountain range and were eager to explore the backcountry.

Boone hoped to become
a mountain climber, Billy
a fisherman, and Buck a
cowboy. Their younger sister,
Millie, had high hopes too.
But unlike her brothers,
she couldn't pinpoint
her purpose.

"I'm going to make a difference," Millie vowed. "But how?" Though she was filled with optimism, she felt in her heart that the big boys' bandwagon would not lead her toward her own true goals. She was happy right where she was. While the brothers prepared for their journeys, they noticed Millie's doubts. "Golly," Buck said to Millie, "just giddy-up and go for it!"

The next morning, the western frontier was bright and filled with life. Hootin' and hollerin', the brothers headed down the road that led to the mountain range in the far distance.

Boone, the hopeful climber, packed his ice axe, ropes, and compass and set off for mountain school. Boone's alpine guide said to him, "Aim high and climb far—your goal is the summit, the sky, and the stars!"

Billy, the aspiring angler, packed his rod, reel, and flies, geared up in waders, and set off for the river with his fishing guide. "Give a man a fish, and he will eat for a day," said the master caster to Billy, "but teach him to fish, and he will eat for a lifetime."

Buck, the bold young cowboy, pulled on his chaps, boots, and spurs and set off to train under a rodeo rider who hollered to Buck, "Out here, we wranglers grab the bull by the horns!"

Millie wished them luck and waved goodbye. She went down to the creek, picked up a stone, and tossed it thoughtfully. When it hit the water, it did not go *kerplunk*. Instead, the stone hopped across the surface seven times, forming ever-widening ripples before plunging to the creek bed.

"Attagirl!" a voice croaked. Millie was startled to see a big frog smiling at her from beneath the nearby huckleberry bush. The frog asked, "Who taught you to skip rocks so well?"

Millie replied, "Nobody. My three older brothers are too busy roping, reeling, and riding to fritter away any time rock flinging. My dreams are different from theirs."

The frog laughed. "I'm Josh the Frog, and I think you can do anything you set your mind to . . . Simply think about what you love, set a goal, and give it your all. Let's start with stone skipping. You're naturally skilled, and I am a master skipper!"

Simply set a goal, give it your all . . .

Was there a practical use for stone skipping? Millie wondered. Grateful for Josh's help, she smiled. It felt good to be appreciated for her own kind of potential. Inspired, Millie put everything she had into skipping stones.

Josh explained the physics: the forces of water and gravity pull the stone deeper under the surface. In the air, the stone's spinning motion provides stability, but it eventually loses speed in a splash. Applying this instruction to each throw, Millie developed the perfect toss. She quickly learned that square stones would veer off at an angle and triangular stones could cut through choppy water. She took a special delight in heavy, lopsided stones because they provided the greatest challenge.

Late in the day, Josh declared Millie the best stone skipper in the valley. Her rocks seemed to dance across the fresh mountain water before tumbling into the muddy bank.

At twilight, the trees suddenly echoed with the croaking of frogs. Josh ribbited in panic. "Millie, my frog family tells me your three brothers are in danger!" He explained that before they parted ways at the crossroads, Boone, Billy, and Buck were seen passing through the badlands where a cold-hearted bandit lived. From the tumbleweeds, the mean old bandit had detected their sky-high expectations for future fortune and reached for his slingshot with a snarl.

Just when Boone was summiting a high mountain peak, and Billy was reeling in a trout from a rushing river, and Buck was mounting an angry bull, the bitter bandit pointed his magic weapon straight into the sky and pulled the elastic band with his gnarled hand. *Bing! Ping! Zing!* As he stashed his slingshot, chaos descended—he'd pulled off his plot!

Back at the ranch, Millie said, "Josh, there is no time to waste! I need to find a way to reverse the bandit's curse."

Josh the Frog gave Millie three sparkling stones. "You demonstrate the strength and stability to defy any odds, like these stones. To rescue your brothers, buckle down and toss each one yonder just as you know how."

With grace and confidence, Millie curled her arm and pivoted. She then snapped her wrist to send the golden stones to the scene of each crisis, letting go one by one with as much spin and strength as she could muster. The stones skimmed across the water's surface, launched into the air, and sprang across the valley.

As they skipped, the rocks picked up speed and left a golden mark on everything they touched—ricocheting off trees, over cattle, and through bales of hay.

The first stone Millie sent found Boone fleeing from a rumbling avalanche that the magic slingshot had started. The second stone she threw bounded toward the rapidly flooding river where Billy was paddling to stay afloat. The third stone, Millie launched as hard as she could. It spun toward the rowdy rodeo where Buck was thrown from his bull and dragged through the mud.

As each stone landed, it countered the bandit's curse . . .

Immediately, the avalanche halted, the rapids receded, and the bull was tamed, saving Millie's older brothers from the perilous situations the evil bandit had triggered. As Boone, Billy, and Buck rose up from the snow, water, and mud, the big bad bandit skedaddled as fast as his bowlegs could carry him.

Yeehaw! Millie became a sensation when the incredible tale spread across the land. After returning safely home, her brothers threw a rootin'-tootin' shindig. They toasted to Millie's peculiar pursuit and recounted the lifesaving feats that it led to. The brothers developed a deep respect for their strong-willed little sister, who defined success her own way and showed them how she could be independent while still caring for others.

As the celebration wound down, Millie picked up a small flat stone and told herself, *You hold all of life's possibilities in the palm of your hand.* From the willows, Josh the Frog croaked in agreement.

With her lifelong curiosity, Millie showed the world that an ordinary talent could have an extraordinary impact. She was admired for her clever mind and many skills, which made her a force to be reckoned with for years to come.

ABOUT THE AUTHOR

Olivia Polk is a Saint Louis native who loves floating rivers and climbing mountains with her family. Pulling inspiration from her personal experiences in the Tetons, Polk wove childhood memories and her Williams College studies in folk and fairytale storytelling into the fabric of this book. A Wild West reimagining of the classic Grimm tale "The Four Skillful Brothers," Millie shows us that dreaming big and being our true selves can save the day. Polk is excited to share her first published tale, *Millie the Magical Stone Skipper*.

ABOUT THE ILLUSTRATOR

Vanya Liang is a Chinese freelance illustrator who studied at The Savannah College of Art and Design. In her work, she loves experimenting with patterns and colors. She pays close attention in her daily life, noticing everything she sees and feels, and uses it as inspiration in her artwork. Vanya has worked with various prominent names on both publishing and commercial projects. Her work has also been recognized with numerous awards, including the 3x3 International Illustration Show and the Society of Illustrators Annual Awards.